For Primrose, who gets into everything.

Little Mouse
Biddle Mouse

paintings & verse by David Kirk

SCHOLASTIC PRESS

CALLAWAY

NEW YORK

Little mouse, Biddle mouse,
Out to explore,
Hunting for tidbits
Across the wide floor.

Such a sweet mousy boy —
What a fine treat,
When you bring breakfast home
For your family to eat!

Glide to the kitchen —
Climb up on the ledge.

Gobble some dainties —
Leap over the edge!

Joy! On the stovetop
There's grease to be licked,
Splatters to sample,
And bones to be picked.

Little mouse, Biddle mouse,
Did you forget?
You haven't put food
In your food basket yet.
Your brothers and sisters
Would like some crumbs, too. . . .

Now there's plenty to spare! Why not sample a few?

Oh my! Biddle mousy,
Just look what you've done.
You ate every bite.
Now your family has none.

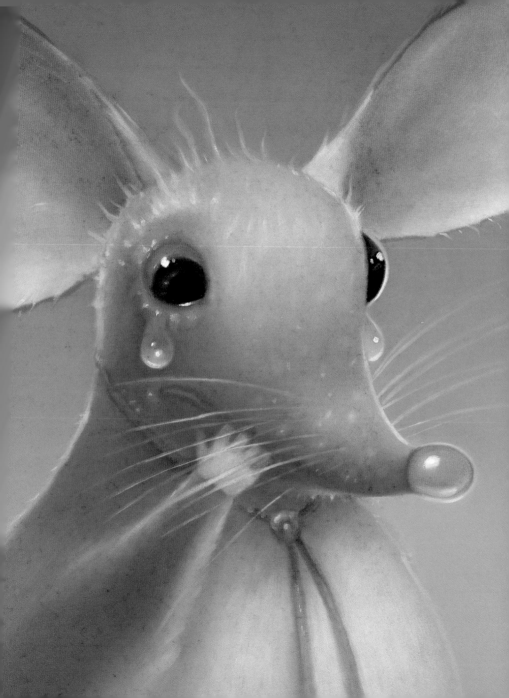

You're so very sorry.
But what can you do?
Perhaps you'd think better
With something to chew!

Bounce to the drain board,
Then visit the sink.
Climb in each glass
To get dribbles to drink.

Hop to the silver drawer —
Lick all the spoons.
Nibble the raisins,
The dates, and the prunes.

Eureka! The cat food —
It's right over there!
With bounty enough
For all mousies to share.

Load up your basket
With beautiful yummies,
To fill all your family's
Bottomless tummies.

Good little Biddle mouse,
How does it feel,
To see your whole family
Enjoying their meal?

The best of mouse pleasures
Is having a feed,
But sharing —
A very close second indeed!

Nicholas Callaway, Editorial Director
Antoinette White, Senior Editor · Sarina Vetterli, Assistant Publisher
George Gould, Production Director · Toshiya Masuda, Senior Designer
Carol Hinz, Associate Editor · Ivan Wong, Jr. and José Rodriguez, Design and Production
With thanks to Jennifer Braunstein at Scholastic Press and Raphael Shea, Art Assistant, at David Kirk's studio.

Library of Congress catalog card number: 00-48489

ISBN 0-439-28051-6

10 9 8 7 6 5 4 3 2 1   02 03 04 05 06

Printed in the U.S.A.
First edition, September 2002

The paintings in this book are oils on paper.

THIS BIDDLE BOOK
BELONGS TO